The Lady Or The Tiger

BY

Frank R. Stockton

ABOUT STOCKTON

Born in Philadelphia in 1834, Frank R. Stockton made a name for himself in American writing by fusing comedy, allegory, and fantasy. Immersed in the vibrant cultural tapestry of 19th-century America, he experimented with a variety of artistic endeavors in his early years before settling down to write. Stockton was originally trained as a wood engraver, thus his move into writing was not only a change of vocation, but a lifelong passion.

Stockton first gained significant attention with the publication of his children's stories and novels, but it was his short story "The Lady, or the Tiger?" that cemented his place as a pioneer of early American fantasy and speculative fiction. Published in 1882, this story became famous for its open-ended conclusion, sparking lively debates among readers and critics alike. This narrative technique, where Stockton left the story's conclusion to the imagination of the reader, became his signature style, showcasing his innovative approach to storytelling.

Beyond his best-known piece, Stockton produced a large and varied body of literature. His books, including "Rudder Grange" and "The Casting Away of Mrs. Lecks and Mrs. Aleshine," satirically portrayed the peculiarities and eccentricities of American culture. His work frequently featured unexpected plot twists and aspects of surprise, which both delighted and occasionally confused his audience.

Stockton's writing style was characterized by a whimsical yet insightful narrative voice. He had a unique ability to weave together the fantastical with the mundane, creating worlds that were both utterly imaginative and strikingly familiar. His stories frequently challenged societal norms and questioned moral dilemmas, making his works timeless and continually relevant.

Throughout his career, Stockton remained at the forefront of literary innovation. He was an esteemed member of the literary community, engaging with other writers and intellectuals of his time. His contributions to children's literature and fantasy are particularly notable for their foresight and creativity, predating and perhaps influencing the later works of authors who explored similar themes.

Stockton passed away in 1902, but his legacy endures. His influence can be seen in the realms of both children's and adult literature, where his pioneering use of the fantasy genre and his narrative style continue to inspire new generations of writers and readers. Through his imaginative prose and engaging storytelling, Frank R. Stockton remains a stalwart figure in the canon of American literature, remembered for his ability to enchant and captivate with the written word.

SUMMARY

This book is presents a gripping and thought-provoking tale that delves into the realms of love, jealousy, and fate. In an ancient kingdom, the king devises a unique method of justice for those accused of a crime: the accused must choose between two doors in an arena, behind one of which awaits a fierce tiger, and behind the other, a beautiful lady whom they must marry if unmarried.

The story centers around a young man, a courtier who has fallen in love with the princess, the king's daughter. When their secret love is discovered, he is thrown into the arena to face the king's grim trial. The princess, aware of what lies behind each door, faces a torturous dilemma—behind one door is a tiger, which would mean a brutal death for her lover, and behind the other, a lady chosen specifically to rival her in beauty, whom her lover would have to marry if he opens her door.

As the courtier looks to the princess for a hint, she subtly signals him towards one door. As he opens it, the story ends abruptly, leaving the readers hanging, forced to wrestle with the mystery: Did the princess let her lover live to be with another, or did jealousy drive her to send him to a violent death? Stockton's tale is a masterful exploration of human nature and the complexities of love, leaving a lasting impression and an unforgettable moral quandary.

CHARACTERS LIST

This book is features a relatively small cast of characters, but each plays a crucial role in the unfolding of the story's central dilemma. Here's a list of the main characters:

The King - He is the ruler of the kingdom and the architect of the unique trial system that involves choosing between two doors. His character is authoritarian and he delights in the absolute power he wields, displaying a kind of poetic justice through the trials in his arena.

The Princess - The king's daughter and the central character, she is portrayed as fiercely passionate and deeply in love with the young man. She is also highly intelligent, willful, and torn between her love for the young man and her jealousy over the possibility of him choosing another woman.

The Young Man - A courtier of the kingdom who falls in love with the princess. His fate becomes the central focus of the story as he is forced to test his luck by choosing between the two doors in the arena, under the watchful eyes of the entire kingdom.

The Lady Behind the Door - She is chosen by the king to be a potential match for the young man should he choose her door. Described as beautiful and fair, she represents the "reward" in the king's twisted system of justice, though she does not actively participate in the story.

The Tiger Behind the Other Door - The tiger symbolizes the deadly penalty of the king's trial. Like the lady, the tiger does not have a personal role in the story but is central to the plot as one of the possible outcomes of the trial.

Each character adds to the intense drama and moral complexity of the story, making "The Lady, or the Tiger?" a compelling study of human nature and emotional conflict.

THE LADY, OR THE TIGER?
By
Frank R. Stockton

In the very olden time there lived a semi-barbaric king, whose

ideas, though somewhat polished and sharpened by the

progressiveness of distant Latin neighbors, were still large,

florid, and untrammeled, as became the half of him which was

barbaric. He was a man of exuberant fancy, and, withal, of an

authority so irresistible that, at his will, he turned his varied

fancies into facts. He was greatly given to self-communing, and,

when he and himself agreed upon anything, the thing was done.

When every member of his domestic and political systems moved

smoothly in its appointed course, his nature was bland and genial;

but, whenever there was a little hitch, and some of his orbs got

out of their orbits, he was blander and more genial still, for

nothing pleased him so much as to make the crooked straight and

crush down uneven places.

Among the borrowed notions by which his barbarism had become

semified was that of the public arena, in which, by exhibitions of

manly and beastly valor, the minds of his subjects were refined

and cultured.

But even here the exuberant and barbaric fancy asserted itself

The arena of the king was built, not to give the people an

opportunity of hearing the rhapsodies of dying gladiators, nor to enable them to view the inevitable conclusion of a conflict

between religious opinions and hungry jaws, but for purposes far

better adapted to widen and develop the mental energies of the

people. This vast amphitheater, with its encircling galleries, its

mysterious vaults, and its unseen passages, was an agent of

poetic justice, in which crime was punished, or virtue rewarded,

by the decrees of an impartial and incorruptible chance.

When a subject was accused of a crime of sufficient importance

to interest the king, public notice was given that on an appointed

day the fate of the accused person would be decided in the king's

arena, a structure which well deserved its name, for, although its

form and plan were borrowed from afar, its purpose emanated

solely from the brain of this man, who, every barleycorn a king, knew no tradition to which he owed more allegiance than pleased

his fancy, and who ingrafted on every adopted form of human

thought and action the rich growth of his barbaric idealism.

When all the people had assembled in the galleries, and the king,

surrounded by his court, sat high up on his throne of royal state

on one side of the arena, he gave a signal, a door beneath him

opened, and the accused subject stepped out into the

amphitheater. Directly opposite him, on the other side of the

inclosed space, were two doors, exactly alike and side by side. It

was the duty and the privilege of the person on trial to walk

directly to these doors and open one of them. He could open either

door he pleased; he was subject to no guidance or influence but

that of the aforementioned impartial and incorruptible chance. If

he opened the one, there came out of it a hungry tiger, the

fiercest and most cruel that could be procured, which

immediately sprang upon him and tore him to pieces as a

punishment for his guilt. The moment that the case of the

criminal was thus decided, doleful iron bells were clanged, great

wails went up from the hired mourners posted on the outer rim of

*the arena, and the vast audience, with bowed heads and downcast

hearts, wended slowly their homeward way, mourning greatly

that one so young and fair, or so old and respected, should have

merited so dire a fate.

But, if the accused person opened the other door, there came forth

from it a lady, the most suitable to his years and station that his

majesty could select among his fair subjects, and to this lady he

was immediately married, as a reward of his innocence. It

mattered not that he might already possess a wife and family, or

that his affections might be engaged upon an object of his own

selection; the king allowed no such subordinate arrangements to

interfere with his great scheme of retribution and reward.

The

exercises, as in the other instance, took place immediately, and

in the arena. Another door opened beneath the king, and a priest,

followed by a band of choristers, and dancing maidens blowing

joyous airs on golden horns and treading an epithalamic measure,

advanced to where the pair stood, side by side, and the wedding

was promptly and cheerily solemnized. Then the gay brass bells

rang forth their merry peals, the people shouted glad hurrahs, and

the innocent man, preceded by children strewing flowers on his

path, led his bride to his home.

This was the king's semi-barbaric method of administering

justice. Its perfect fairness is obvious. The criminal could not

know out of which door would come the lady; he opened either he pleased, without having the slightest idea whether, in the next

instant, he was to be devoured or married. On some occasions the

tiger came out of one door, and on some out of the other. The

decisions of this tribunal were not only fair, they were positively

determinate: the accused person was instantly punished if he

found himself guilty, and, if innocent, he was rewarded on the

spot, whether he liked it or not. There was no escape from the

judgments of the king's arena.

The institution was a very popular one. When the people gathered

together on one of the great trial days, they never knew whether

they were to witness a bloody slaughter or a hilarious wedding.

This element of uncertainty lent an interest to the occasion

which it could not otherwise have attained. Thus, the masses

were entertained and pleased, and the thinking part of the

community could bring no charge of unfairness against this
plan,

for did not the accused person have the whole matter in his
own

hands?

This semi-barbaric king had a daughter as blooming as his
most

florid fancies, and with a soul as fervent and imperious as his

own. As is usual in such cases, she was the apple of his eye,
and

was loved by him above all humanity. Among his courtiers
was a

young man of that fineness of blood and lowness of station

common to the conventional heroes of romance who love
royal

maidens. This royal maiden was well satisfied with her lover,
for

he was handsome and brave to a degree unsurpassed in all
this

kingdom, and she loved him with an ardor that had enough of

barbarism in it to make it exceedingly warm and strong.

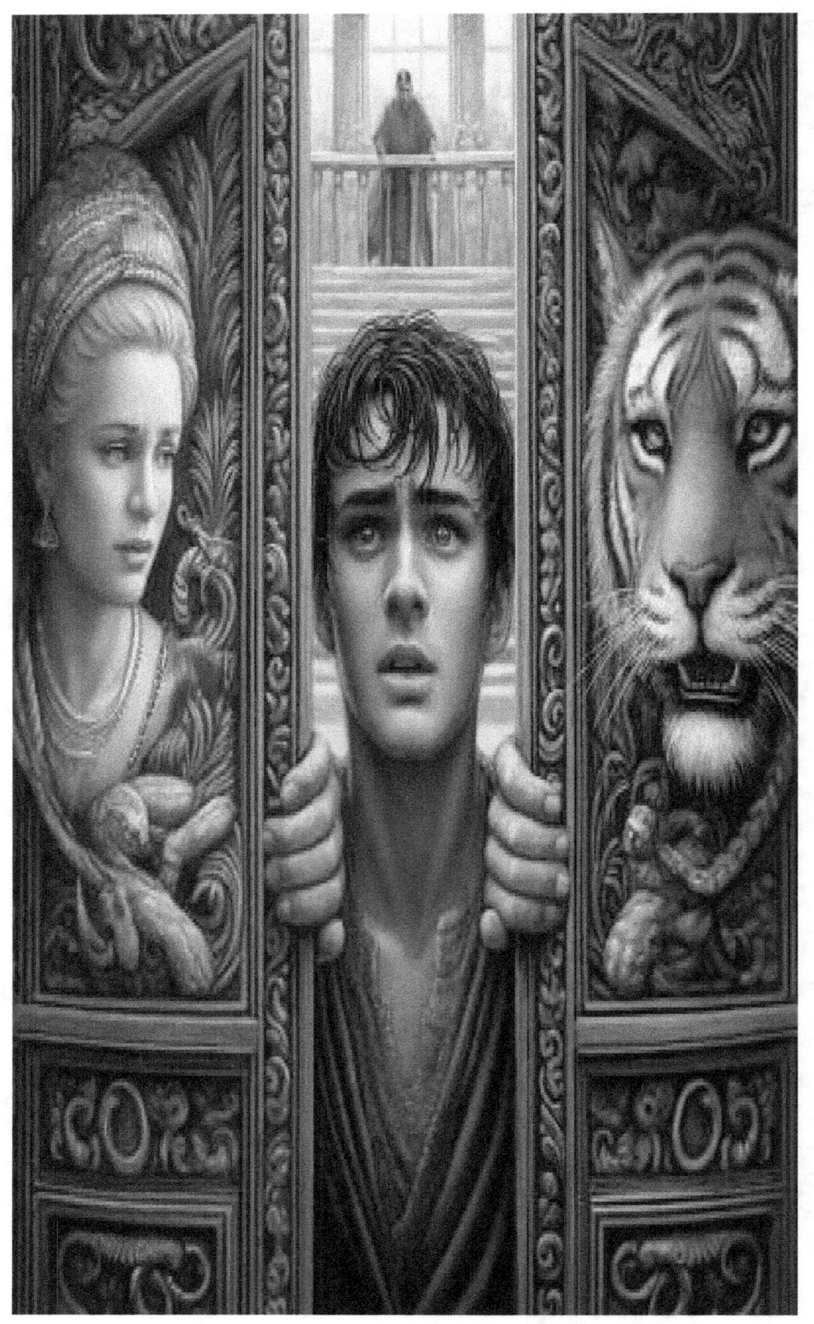

This love

affair moved on happily for many months, until one day the king

happened to discover its existence. He did not hesitate nor waver

in regard to his duty in the premises. The youth was immediately

cast into prison, and a day was appointed for his trial in the

king's arena. This, of course, was an especially important

occasion, and his majesty, as well as all the people, was greatly

interested in the workings and development of this trial.

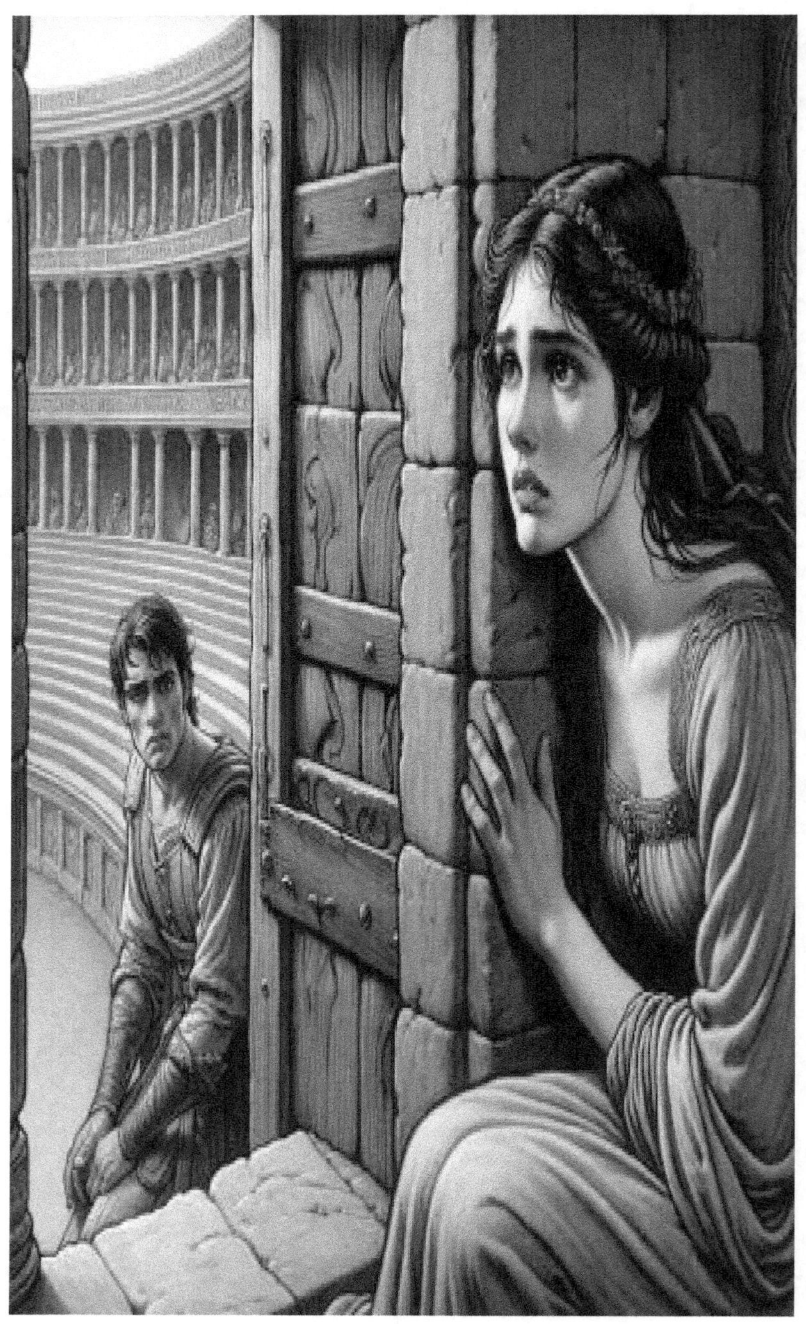

Never

before had such a case occurred; never before had a subject dared

to love the daughter of the king. In after years such things

became commonplace enough, but then they were in no slight

degree novel and startling.

The tiger-cages of the kingdom were searched for the most

savage and relentless beasts, from which the fiercest monster

might be selected for the arena; and the ranks of maiden youth

and beauty throughout the land were carefully surveyed by

competent judges in order that the young man might have a

fitting bride in case fate did not determine for him a different

destiny. Of course, everybody knew that the deed with which the

accused was charged had been done. He had loved the princess, and

neither he, she, nor any one else, thought of denying the fact; but

the king would not think of allowing any fact of this kind to interfere with the workings of the tribunal, in which he took such

great delight and satisfaction.

No matter how the affair turned

out, the youth would be disposed of, and the king would take an

aesthetic pleasure in watching the course of events, which would

determine whether or not the young man had done wrong in

allowing himself to love the princess.

The appointed day arrived. From far and near the people gathered,

and thronged the great galleries of the arena, and crowds, unable

to gain admittance, massed themselves against its outside walls.

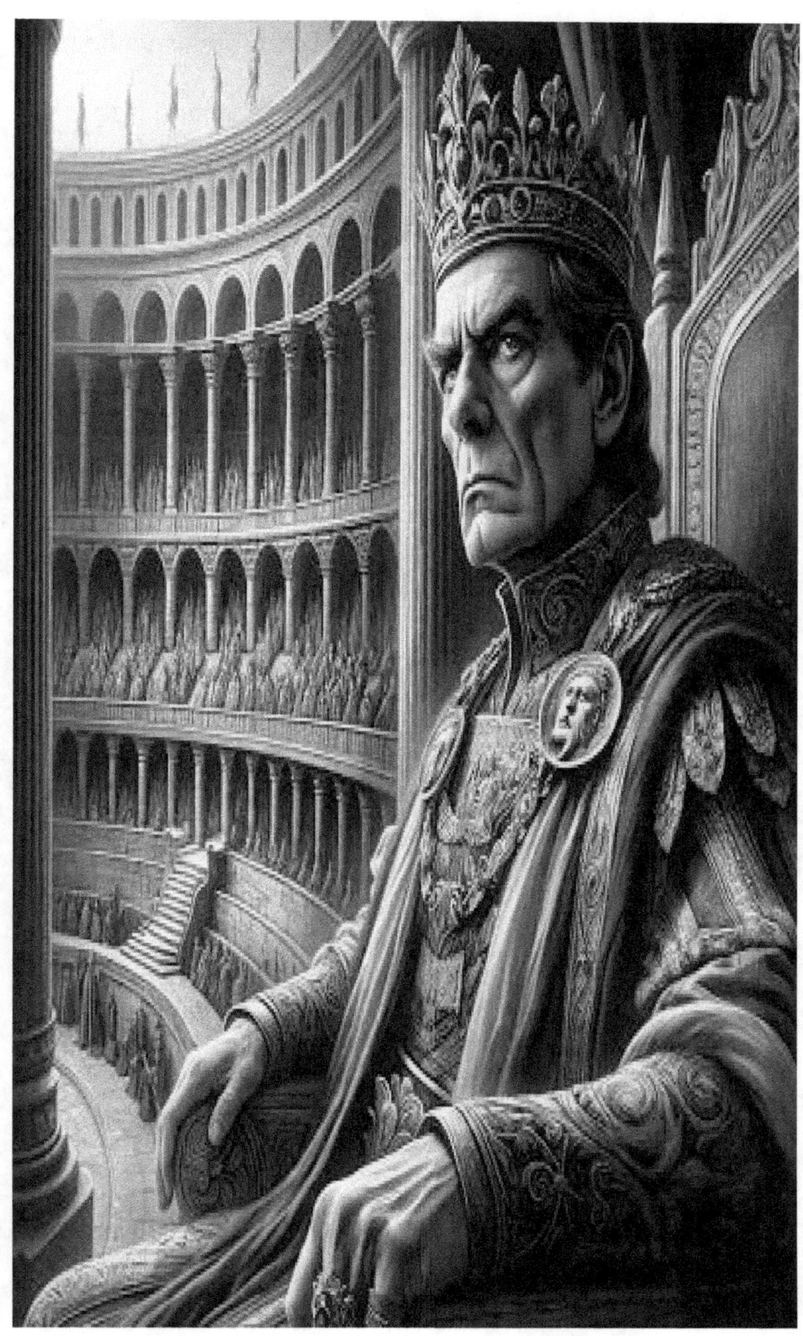

The king and his court were in their places, opposite the twin

doors, those fateful portals, so terrible in their similarity.

All was ready. The signal was given. A door beneath the royal

party opened, and the lover of the princess walked into the arena.

Tall, beautiful, fair, his appearance was greeted with a low hum

of admiration and anxiety. Half the audience had not known so

grand a youth had lived among them. No wonder the princess loved

him! What a terrible thing for him to be there!

As the youth advanced into the arena he turned, as the custom

was, to bow to the king, but he did not think at all of that royal

personage. His eyes were fixed upon the princess, who sat to the

right of her father. Had it not been for the moiety of barbarism in her nature it is probable that lady would not have been there, but

her intense and fervid soul would not allow her to be absent on an

occasion in which she was so terribly interested. From the

moment that the decree had gone forth that her lover should

decide his fate in the king's arena, she had thought of nothing,

night or day, but this great event and the various subjects

connected with it. Possessed of more power, influence, and force

of character than any one who had ever before been interested in

such a case, she had done what no other person had done,— she had

possessed herself of the secret of the doors. She knew in which

of the two rooms, that lay behind those doors, stood the cage of

the tiger, with its open front, and in which waited the lady.

Through these thick doors, heavily curtained with skins on the

inside, it was impossible that any noise or suggestion should

come from within to the person who should approach to raise the

latch of one of them. But gold, and the power of a woman's will,

had brought the secret to the princess.

And not only did she know in which room stood the lady ready to

emerge, all blushing and radiant, should her door be opened, but

she knew who the lady was.

It was one of the fairest and

loveliest of the damsels of the court who had been selected as

the reward of the accused youth, should he be proved innocent of

the crime of aspiring to one so far above him; and the princess

hated her. Often had she seen, or imagined that she had seen, this

fair creature throwing glances of admiration upon the person of

her lover, and sometimes she thought these glances were

perceived, and even returned. Now and then she had seen them

talking together; it was but for a moment or two, but much can be

said in a brief space; it may have been on most unimportant

topics, but how could she know that? The girl was lovely, but she

had dared to raise her eyes to the loved one of the princess; and,

with all the intensity of the savage blood transmitted to her

through long lines of wholly barbaric ancestors, she hated the

woman who blushed and trembled behind that silent door.

When her lover turned and looked at her, and his eye met hers as

she sat there, paler and whiter than any one in the vast ocean of

anxious faces about her, he saw, by that power of quick

perception which is given to those whose souls are one, that she

knew behind which door crouched the tiger, and behind which

stood the lady. He had expected her to know it. He understood her

nature, and his soul was assured that she would never rest until

she had made plain to herself this thing, hidden to all other

lookers-on, even to the king. The only hope for the youth in which

there was any element of certainty was based upon the success

of the princess in discovering this mystery; and the moment he

looked upon her, he saw she had succeeded, as in his soul he knew

she would succeed.

Then it was that his quick and anxious glance asked the question:

"Which?" It was as plain to her as if he shouted it from where he

stood. There was not an instant to be lost. The question was

asked in a flash; it must be answered in another.

Her right arm lay on the cushioned parapet before her.

She raised

her hand, and made a slight, quick movement toward the
right. No

one but her lover saw her. Every eye but his was fixed on the
man

in the arena.

He turned, and with a firm and rapid step he walked across
the

empty space. Every heart stopped beating, every breath was
held,

every eye was fixed immovably upon that man. Without the

slightest hesitation, he went to the door on the right, and
opened

it.

Now, the point of the story is this: Did the tiger come out of that

door, or did the lady ?

The more we reflect upon this question, the harder it is to

answer. It involves a study of the human heart which leads us

through devious mazes of passion, out of which it is difficult to

find our way. Think of it, fair reader, not as if the decision of the

question depended upon yourself, but upon that hot-blooded,

semi-barbaric princess, her soul at a white heat beneath the

combined fires of despair and jealousy. She had lost him, but who

should have him?

How often, in her waking hours and in her dreams, had she started

in wild horror, and covered her face with her hands as she thought

of her lover opening the door on the other side of which waited the cruel fangs of the tiger!

But how much oftener had she seen him at the other door!

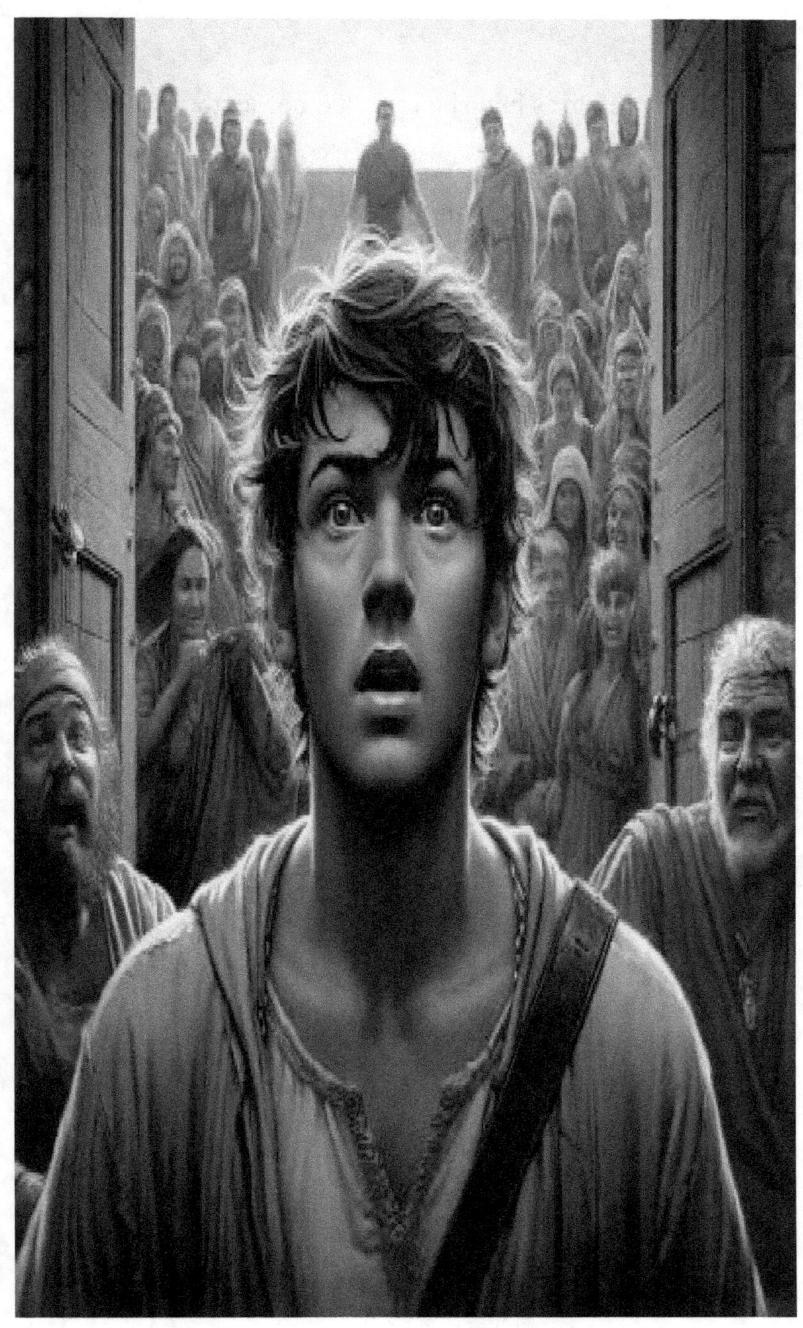

How in

her grievous reveries had she gnashed her teeth, and torn her hair,

when she saw his start of rapturous delight as he opened the door

of the lady! How her soul had burned in agony when she had seen

him rush to meet that woman, with her flushing cheek and

sparkling eye of triumph; when she had seen him lead her forth,

his whole frame kindled with the joy of recovered life; when she

had heard the glad shouts from the multitude, and the wild

ringing of the happy bells; when she had seen the priest, with his

joyous followers, advance to the couple, and make them man and

wife before her very eyes; and when she had seen

them walk away together upon their path of flowers, followed by

the tremendous shouts of the hilarious multitude, in which her

one despairing shriek was lost and drowned!

Would it not be better for him to die at once, and go to wait for

her in the blessed regions of semi-barbaric futurity?

And yet, that awful tiger, those shrieks, that blood!

Her decision had been indicated in an instant, but it had been

made after days and nights of anguished deliberation. She had

known she would be asked, she had decided what she would

answer, and, without the slightest hesitation, she had moved her

hand to the right.

The question of her decision is one not to be lightly considered,

and it is not for me to presume to set myself up as the one person

able to answer it. And so I leave it with all of you: Which came

out of the opened door,—the lady, or the tiger?

THE END